Little
Big Giant

Stories of Wisdom and Inspiration

1

Introduction

As the sun set over the bustling streets of Vienna, a young Wolfgang Amadeus Mozart sat at his piano, his fingers dancing effortlessly across the keys. The notes that flowed from his instrument were like magic, captivating all who heard them. But little did anyone know, this was just the beginning of the musical genius that would change the world forever.

Table of Contents

Chapter 1

Early Years: Childhood Prodigy

Wolfgang Amadeus Mozart was born on January 27, 1756 in Salzburg, Austria. He was the youngest of seven children and from a very young age, it was clear that he was a special child. His father, Leopold Mozart, was a successful composer and violinist and recognized his son's talent early on.

As a child, Mozart showed a natural inclination towards music. He was able to play simple melodies on the keyboard at the age of three and by the time he was five, he was composing his own music. His father, amazed by his son's abilities, started teaching him music theory and the violin.

Mozart's childhood was filled with music. He spent hours practicing and perfecting his skills. His father took him on tours around Europe, showcasing his talent to the public. Everywhere they went, people were amazed by the young Mozart's abilities. He was a true prodigy.

At the age of six, Mozart and his family traveled to Vienna, where he performed for the royal family. Empress Maria Theresa was so impressed by his skills that she declared him a "miracle child." This was just the beginning of Mozart's rise to fame.

Despite his young age, Mozart was able to compose complex pieces of music. His father would give him a theme and he would create a masterpiece out of it. His compositions were full of emotion and showed a deep understanding of music.

But it wasn't just music that Mozart excelled in. He was also a skilled linguist, speaking several languages including German, Italian, and French. He was also an avid reader and had a vast knowledge of literature and history.

Key Takeaway: Mozart's early years show us that with hard work, dedication, and a natural talent, anything is possible. He was able to achieve greatness at a young age because he put in the time and effort to hone his skills. It's important to never give up on our passions and to always strive for excellence.

12

Chapter 2

Musical Education and Early Compositions

Wolfgang Amadeus Mozart was a musical prodigy, meaning he showed incredible talent and skill at a very young age. His father, Leopold Mozart, was a musician and recognized his son's musical abilities from a very young age. Leopold decided to give Wolfgang and his older sister, Maria Anna, musical education at home.

At the age of 3, Wolfgang began learning how to play the harpsichord, a keyboard instrument popular during that time period. He was a quick learner and could play simple pieces by the age of 5. Leopold was amazed by his son's musical abilities and decided to take him and his sister on a tour of Europe to showcase their talents.

The Mozart family traveled to cities like Vienna, Paris, and London, where Wolfgang and Maria Anna performed for kings, queens, and other important people. People were amazed by the young Mozart's skills and were often left in awe after his performances. He was even nicknamed

"The Little Wonder" by the Empress of Austria.

During their travels, Leopold made sure that Wolfgang and Maria Anna continued their musical education. They studied with some of the best musicians in Europe, learning about different styles of music and how to compose their own pieces. Wolfgang was particularly interested in the works of Johann Sebastian Bach and George Frideric Handel.

At the age of 8, Wolfgang composed his first symphony, which is a musical piece for an orchestra. It was called "Symphony No. 1 in E flat major" and showed his incredible talent and understanding of music at such a young age. He also composed other pieces like sonatas and concertos, which are musical pieces for a solo instrument and orchestra.

Key Takeaway: Even at a young age, Wolfgang Amadeus Mozart showed incredible talent and dedication to his musical education. He was constantly learning and improving his skills, which helped him become one of the greatest composers in history. It's important to never stop learning and to always strive for improvement in whatever you are passionate about.

Chapter 3

European Tour and Rise to Fame

After his successful performance in Vienna, young Wolfgang Amadeus Mozart was invited to go on a grand tour of Europe. At only six years old, he was already making a name for himself in the music world.

His first stop was in Munich, Germany, where he performed for the Elector of Bavaria. The Elector was so impressed with Mozart's talent that he offered to take him under his wing and provide him with a proper musical education. However,

Mozart's father, Leopold, wanted to continue traveling and showcasing his son's abilities to the rest of Europe.

Next, they traveled to Paris, France, where Mozart's performances were met with mixed reviews. Some were amazed by his skills, while others criticized him for being too young to be a serious musician. But Mozart didn't let the negative comments bring him down. He continued to practice and improve his craft, determined to prove his critics wrong.

The family then made their way to London, England, where Mozart's talent truly shone. He performed for the royal family and received high praise from King George III himself. He also composed his first symphony during his time in London, which was met with great success.

As they continued their tour, Mozart's fame grew, and he became known as a child prodigy. He was invited to perform for nobility and even met with other famous musicians, such as Johann Christian Bach, who became his mentor.

Despite his young age, Mozart's musical genius was undeniable. He was able to compose music effortlessly and perform with incredible skill and emotion. His European tour not only showcased his talents but also allowed him to learn from other great musicians and further develop his craft.

Key Takeaway: Even at a young age, Mozart's determination and passion for music led him to great success. He didn't let criticism or setbacks discourage him, and instead, he used them as motivation to become an even better musician. This teaches us that with hard work and perseverance, we can achieve our goals and dreams.

Chapter 4

Struggles and Controversies

As Wolfgang Amadeus Mozart's fame and talent grew, so did the struggles and controversies in his life. Despite his incredible musical abilities, Mozart faced many challenges and obstacles throughout his career.

One of the biggest struggles for Mozart was financial stability. Despite being a renowned composer, he often struggled to make ends meet. His lavish lifestyle and extravagant spending habits often left him in debt. Mozart also faced difficulty finding steady employment, as he often clashed with his employers and had a reputation for being unreliable.

In addition to financial struggles, Mozart also faced controversies within the music community. Many of his fellow composers were envious of his talent and success, leading to tension and rivalries. Some even went as far as to spread rumors and gossip about Mozart, trying to discredit his work.

Another major controversy in Mozart's life was his relationship with his father, Leopold. While Leopold had been a supportive and encouraging figure in Mozart's early career, their relationship became strained as Mozart grew older. Leopold often interfered in Mozart's personal and professional life, causing tension and arguments between them.

Despite these struggles and controversies, Mozart continued to compose and perform. He faced criticism and setbacks, but his passion for music never wavered. Even when facing financial difficulties and personal conflicts, Mozart poured his heart and soul into his music, creating some of his most iconic pieces.

Key Takeaway: Even the most talented and successful individuals face struggles and controversies in their lives. It's important to stay true to yourself and your passions, even when facing challenges and criticism. Mozart's determination and dedication to his music serve as an inspiration for us all.

Chapter 5

Marriage and Family Life

Wolfgang Amadeus Mozart was not only a musical genius, but he was also a loving husband and father. At the young age of 26, Mozart married Constanze Weber, a talented singer. They had first met when Mozart was just 21 and Constanze was only 16. Despite their age difference, they fell deeply in love and were married in a beautiful ceremony surrounded by their family and friends.

Mozart and Constanze's marriage was not always easy. Mozart's career as a composer and musician kept him very busy, often traveling for performances and working long hours. But Constanze was a devoted wife and supported her husband's passion for music. She even helped him with his work, copying his compositions and managing his finances.

Together, Mozart and Constanze had six children, but unfortunately, only two survived infancy. Their first child, Raimund Leopold, was born in 1783 and their second child, Karl Thomas, was born in 1784.

Tragically, both boys passed away within a year of their births. Despite the heartache of losing their children, Mozart and Constanze remained strong and leaned on each other for support.

In 1787, their third child, a daughter named Anna Maria, was born. She was followed by three more sons: Franz Xaver in 1791, Karl Thomas in 1792, and Johann Thomas in 1796. Mozart loved his children dearly and often wrote songs and pieces for them to sing and play. He even dedicated some of his compositions to them, showing his love and pride for his family.

Mozart and Constanze's marriage was not without its challenges. Mozart's constant financial struggles and his love for partying and gambling caused some strain in their relationship. But through it all, they remained committed to each other and their family.

Sadly, Mozart's life was cut short at the young age of 35. He passed away in 1791, leaving behind his beloved wife and children. Constanze, with the help of Mozart's friends and colleagues, worked tirelessly to preserve his legacy and ensure that his music would continue to be played and appreciated for generations to come.

Key Takeaway: Marriage and family are important aspects of life, even for the most talented and successful individuals. Mozart's love for his wife and children showed that even in the midst of his busy career, he valued his family above all else. And despite the challenges they faced, their love and support for each other never wavered.

Chapter 6

Musical Innovations and Masterpieces

Wolfgang Amadeus Mozart was a true musical genius. His talent and passion for music were evident from a young age, and he continued to amaze the world with his musical innovations and masterpieces throughout his short but impactful life.

One of Mozart's most significant contributions to music was his development of the symphony. During his time, the symphony was typically a three-movement piece, but Mozart expanded it to four movements, adding a minuet and trio section. He also incorporated a greater range of instruments and musical techniques, creating a more dynamic and complex sound. His symphonies, such as "Symphony No. 40 in G Minor" and "Symphony No. 41 in C Major," are still revered as some of the greatest works in classical music.

In addition to his symphonies, Mozart also revolutionized the opera genre. He wrote over 20 operas, including "The Marriage of Figaro" and "Don Giovanni," which are considered some of the most brilliant and influential operas of all time. Mozart's operas featured complex and emotional storylines, beautiful melodies, and intricate vocal harmonies. He also introduced new elements, such as ensemble pieces and arias with multiple characters, which added depth and complexity to his operas.

Mozart's mastery of the piano was also unparalleled. He was a child prodigy on the instrument, and his skills only continued to grow as he matured. He composed over 600 pieces for the piano, including sonatas, concertos, and variations. His piano works showcased his technical prowess and creativity, with intricate fingerings, complex rhythms, and unexpected harmonies. Some of his most famous piano pieces include "Piano Sonata No. 11 in A Major" and "Piano Concerto No. 21 in C Major."

Aside from his musical innovations, Mozart also created many masterpieces that have stood the test of time. His "Requiem Mass in D Minor" is one of the most famous and beloved choral works in history. It was his final composition, left unfinished at his untimely death, but completed by his students and colleagues.

The "Requiem" is a haunting and powerful piece, with soaring melodies and emotional depth that continues to move listeners to this day.

Another one of Mozart's masterpieces is his "Eine Kleine Nachtmusik" or "A Little Night Music." This serenade is one of his most popular and recognizable works, with its joyful and lively melodies. It has been used in countless films, commercials, and other media, solidifying its place as one of the most iconic pieces of classical music.

Key Takeaway: Mozart's musical innovations and masterpieces have left an indelible mark on the world of music. His contributions to the symphony, opera, piano, and choral music have shaped the way we understand and appreciate classical music today. Through his creativity and talent, Mozart continues to inspire and captivate audiences of all ages.

Chapter 7

Decline in Popularity and Financial

Struggles

As Wolfgang Amadeus Mozart grew older, he faced many challenges that affected his career and personal life. Despite his immense talent and success in his early years, he began to experience a decline in popularity and financial struggles.

One of the main reasons for this decline was the changing tastes of the public. During Mozart's time, music was becoming more serious and complex, and his light and playful compositions were not as popular as they once were. This led to fewer people attending his concerts and buying his music, causing a decrease in his income.

Additionally, Mozart's extravagant lifestyle and love for expensive things also contributed to his financial struggles. He enjoyed living a lavish life, wearing expensive clothes and throwing extravagant parties. However, this lifestyle was not sustainable, and Mozart soon found himself in debt.

To make matters worse, Mozart's health began to decline, and he suffered from various illnesses, including severe headaches and fevers. This affected his ability to compose and perform, leading to a decrease in the quality of his work.

Despite these challenges, Mozart continued to compose and perform, but he was not receiving the recognition and financial stability he deserved. He even had to borrow money from friends and family to support himself and his family.

Sadly, Mozart's financial struggles and declining popularity took a toll on his mental health. He became increasingly stressed and anxious, and this affected his relationships with his family and friends. He also started to doubt his own abilities as a composer, which further impacted his work.

Key Takeaway: Even the most talented and successful individuals can face challenges and struggles in their lives. It is essential to manage one's finances and prioritize mental and physical well-being to maintain a successful and fulfilling career.

Chapter 8

Final Years and Legacy

As Mozart entered his final years, he continued to compose and perform, but his health was declining. He suffered from frequent illnesses and financial struggles, which put a strain on his family. Despite these challenges, Mozart remained dedicated to his music and his legacy continued to grow.

During this time, Mozart composed some of his most famous works, including "The Magic Flute" and his final masterpiece,

"Requiem." He also traveled extensively, performing in front of royalty and gaining even more recognition for his talents.

However, as Mozart's health deteriorated, he became more and more reliant on his wife, Constanze, to handle his business affairs. Unfortunately, she was not as skilled in managing finances as Mozart was in composing music. This led to financial difficulties for the family and added stress to Mozart's already fragile health.

In 1791, at the young age of 35, Mozart passed away. His death was a shock to the music world, and many mourned the loss of such a talented and influential composer. It was later revealed that Mozart had died from a severe illness, possibly caused by overworking himself.

Despite his untimely death, Mozart's legacy continued to live on. His music remained popular and influential, and his name became synonymous with genius and creativity. Many composers and musicians were inspired by Mozart's works, and his influence can still be seen in music today.

Key Takeaway: Mozart's final years were filled with both triumphs and struggles. He continued to create beautiful music despite his declining health and financial difficulties. His legacy lives on, and his impact on the world of music will never be forgotten.

Chapter 9

Influence on Classical Music

Wolfgang Amadeus Mozart was not only a musical genius, but he also had a huge impact on the world of classical music. His compositions were revolutionary and changed the way people thought about music. Let's explore how Mozart's influence can still be felt in the world of classical music today.

Mozart's Music Style

Mozart's music was known for its elegance, beauty, and complexity. He was a master of composing melodies that were both catchy and emotional. His use of different instruments and harmonies created a unique sound that was different from any other composer of his time.

Mozart's music was also known for its technical skill. He was able to write complex pieces with ease, showing off his incredible talent and mastery of the piano and other instruments. His music was not only pleasing to the ear, but it also challenged and inspired other composers to push the boundaries of classical music.

Influence on Other Composers

Mozart's impact on classical music can be seen through the influence he had on other composers. His music inspired many great composers, such as Ludwig van Beethoven and Franz Schubert. Beethoven, in particular, was heavily influenced by Mozart's use of melodies and harmonies, which can be heard in his own compositions.

Mozart's music also influenced the development of the classical style. His works were a bridge between the Baroque and Classical periods, and his use of classical forms, such as the sonata and concerto, helped to shape the future of classical music.

Impact on Music Education

Mozart's influence can also be seen in the world of music education. His compositions are often used as teaching tools for young musicians to learn about classical music. His works are not only technically challenging but also emotionally engaging, making them perfect for students to study and learn from.

Many music schools and conservatories also have Mozart's pieces as part of their curriculum, showcasing his lasting impact on classical music education. His music continues to inspire and teach new generations of musicians, keeping his legacy alive.

Key Takeaway

Wolfgang Amadeus Mozart's influence on classical music cannot be overstated. His music style, impact on other composers, and influence on music education have made him one of the most significant figures in the history of classical music. His compositions continue to be admired and studied, and his legacy lives on through the music he left behind.

Through his work, Mozart showed us the power of music to touch our hearts and minds. He proved that with hard work and dedication, one can achieve greatness and leave a lasting impact on the world. So, let us all be inspired by Mozart's music and strive to create something beautiful and meaningful, just like he did.

Chapter 10

*Remembering Mozart: Celebrating his Life
and Music*

Wolfgang Amadeus Mozart was a musical genius who lived during the 18th century. He was born in Salzburg, Austria in 1756 and showed a love for music at a very young age. His father, Leopold Mozart, was a musician and composer himself and recognized his son's talent early on. He began teaching Mozart how to play the harpsichord when he was just three years old.

Mozart's talent was extraordinary and he quickly became known as a child prodigy. He was able to play the piano and violin with ease and could even compose his own music by the time he was five years old. People were amazed by his skills and he began performing in front of audiences at a very young age.

As Mozart grew older, his talent only continued to blossom. He composed hundreds of pieces of music, including symphonies, concertos, and operas. His music was loved by many and he became a famous composer throughout Europe. He even performed for kings and queens, gaining the title of "royal musician."

Despite his success, Mozart faced many challenges in his life. He struggled with money and often had to rely on others for financial support. He also faced criticism from other composers who were jealous of his talent. But through it all, Mozart continued to create beautiful music that touched the hearts of many.

Sadly, Mozart's life was cut short at the young age of 35. He passed away in 1791, leaving behind a legacy of incredible music that still lives on today. His compositions continue to be studied and performed by musicians all over the world.

Key Takeaway: Mozart's passion for music and determination to follow his dreams is an inspiration to us all. Despite facing challenges, he never gave up and his legacy lives on through his beautiful music.

Dear Reader,

Thank you for choosing "Little Big Giant - Stories of Wisdom and Inspiration"! We hope this book has inspired and motivated you on your own journey to success.

If you enjoyed reading this book and believe in the power of its message, we kindly ask for your support. Please consider leaving a positive review on the platform where you purchased the book. Your review will help spread the message to more young readers, empowering them to dream big and achieve greatness. We acknowledge that mistakes can happen, and we appreciate your forgiveness.

Remember, the overall message of this book is the key. Thank you for being a part of our mission to inspire and uplift young minds.

Made in United States
Orlando, FL
18 December 2024

56021215R00046